DORRIE and the WIZARD'S SPELL

by Patricia Coombs

Lothrop, Lee & Shepard Co., Inc., New York

FOR

DAWN

AND

DAVID

This is Dorrie. She is a witch. A little witch. Her hat is always crooked and her socks never match. The Big Witch is her mother, and Gink is her very own black cat.

One Monday Cook was away and Dorrie was trying to think of something to do, when the Big Witch said:

"I need someone to help me at the Library Bazaar and Tea today. Do you think you and Gink could help?"

"Oh yes," said Dorrie. "I would like that."
Dorrie ran and got her cloak and put it on, and Gink went with her.

The Big Witch tied a sack of things for the Sale
to the broomstick. Dorrie and Gink climbed on the
broomstick behind the Big Witch and they flew
into the air.

Over the house and trees they went, over the marsh
and the pond toward town.

They landed in front of the library right beside
a big sign that read:
"BAZAAR AND TEA TODAY."

A Wizard named Wink was just landing, too.
They said "HOWDOYOUDO" and went inside.

Dorrie helped the Big Witch put everything out on a long table. There were plates and vases and plants, and bats and balloons and boxes of toads. There were mittens and scarves and skates, and hats and ladles and lace.

In another room there was a big sign that read:
"TEA PARTY IN HERE."

All the books that began with *W* were in there.
Most of them were *Wicked* or *Witches* or *Wizards*
or *Worse*.

"I like selling things," said Dorrie.

"And the library will soon have enough money to buy a new glue cauldron," said the Big Witch, "and another broomstick holder for the hall."

Suddenly Wink the Wizard jumped up beside Dorrie. "PSSST!" he whispered to her, "I have something special for you to sell. It is the strongest Magic I ever thought up."

Wink the Wizard reached up his sleeve and pulled out a little jar. He put it down beside Dorrie, and before she could ask what sort of magic it was, Wink the Wizard disappeared in the crowd.

Dinger and Squig came. Dorrie showed Dinger an alarm clock.

"I love alarm clocks!" shouted Dinger. "I will buy it. Now I have seventy-three alarm clocks."

Dinger was so happy he danced around to the ringing of the alarm clock.

Squig chased Dinger around the room, waving his umbrella at him until Dinger turned the clock off.

Miss Dorp bought a whole box
of scarves and gloves
and beads and bracelets and bangles.

Squig came back and got a pair
of yellow earmuffs to wear
in case Dinger started ringing his
alarm clock again.

Then he bought three umbrellas.

Mr. Obs came by to get
new violin strings and a
pair of red mittens.

Crowds of witches Dorrie had never seen before came and went, muttering and mumbling and fighting over all the things on the table.

Wizards hurried around with bags and boxes of things they had bought.

Dorrie was very, very busy. The Big Witch was very, very busy.

Soon nearly everything was gone.

The Big Witch sat down and sighed. "My goodness, I am tired. And I think I am getting a headache. Dorrie, bring me a cup of tea and I will take my headache powder."

"All right, Mother," said Dorrie. She skipped
past the chattering witches and wizards into the Tea
Party Room. Gink went with her.

Mr. Obs was pouring tea and wearing his new
red mittens.

"Your mittens look very nice, Mr. Obs," said
Dorrie. "May I please have a cup of tea for
Mother?"

Mr. Obs poured a cup of tea. Dorrie carried it very carefully back across the room to the Big Witch.

"Thank you," said the Big Witch. "Now, if I can just find my headache powder. The jar was right here a minute ago."

Dorrie and the Big Witch looked all around.

"Oh my," said Dorrie, "maybe I sold it."

"Hmmmm," said the Big Witch, "no, here it is."

The Big Witch put the powder into her tea and slowly drank it.

Dorrie sold two jars of thistle jam, a blue plate, and a speckled bat. She helped a nice fat witch who could not see very well find a pair of glasses. They were sunglasses, but the fat witch loved them.

Dorrie turned around to show the Big Witch how many things she had sold. Nearly everything was gone.

So was the Big Witch.

"Mother?" said Dorrie. She looked all around. She looked under the table.

The Big Witch wasn't there.

"I wonder what happened to Mother, Gink," said Dorrie.

Gink blinked and meowed.

Some funny-looking witches came over to Dorrie.

"Pssst!" said one, "we heard that Wizard Wink left a spell for sale here. We'll buy it."

"Oh," said Dorrie, "I forgot all about that. It's around here some place." She found the little jar behind a broken teapot and gave it to the witches. They began to fight and screech over it. One of them snatched it and the top flew off. The powder scattered all over them.

One witch stuck out her tongue and tasted the powder.

"Bah! A trick!" she cried. "It is nothing but head-ache powder!"

The witches rushed off angrily.

Dorrie picked up the little jar and looked at it.

"Headache powder? But Mother . . . oh no! Oh, Gink, Mother took the wrong powder with her tea!"

Dorrie ran across the room. She ran into the Tea Party Room and Gink went with her. She looked all over for Wink the Wizard.

She looked and looked and looked. Finally she saw him sitting on a shelf.

"Wizard Wink," said Dorrie, "my mother has disappeared. She drank the spell in the bottle you left, instead of her headache powder."

Wink the Wizard laughed. He laughed and laughed and laughed so hard he tumbled off the shelf.

Dorrie was cross.

"Please hurry and tell me what was in that spell. I have to find my mother."

Wink the Wizard stopped laughing just long enough to say:

"It turns witches into whatever they are looking at when they drink it. Isn't that clever? The Big Witch will now be a string of beads, or an alarm clock, or a speckled bat for the next thousand years!"

Wink the Wizard vanished in a puff of smoke.

"Oh, Gink," said Dorrie, "we sold Mother to somebody at the Bazaar. We have to find her. But first, I have to remember what Mother was looking at when we gave her the cup of tea. Oh my."

Dorrie went to Mr. Obs.

"Mr. Obs!" said Dorrie, "something awful has happened to Mother. Somebody bought her by mistake."

Mr. Obs dropped his violin. Miss Dorp and Squig and Dinger rushed over to see what was wrong. Dorrie told them how the Big Witch drank the Wizard's spell.

"Hmmmm," said Dinger, "do you think my new alarm clock is the Big Witch?"

They all looked at the alarm clock very hard.

"I don't think so," said Dorrie. "You had already bought the clock when Mother disappeared."

"Ah," said Mr. Obs, "perhaps she is a violin string, or my new red mittens!"

"Or my beads!" cried Miss Dorp, swinging a string of beads in the air. The string broke and the beads rolled all over the floor.

"Oh, I hope that isn't Mother!" wailed Dorrie.

"Now, now," said Mr. Obs, "don't worry. We will be very quiet and THINK. What was the Big Witch looking at when Dorrie gave her the cup of tea?"

They all stood still and thought very hard.

"Well," said Dorrie, "I think Mother must have been looking at the cup of tea."

"Hmmmm," said Squig, "if that is so, then the Big Witch drank herself, and we will never find her."

Dinger grabbed one of Squig's umbrellas and pulled it down over Squig's head.

"KEEP STILL! It isn't the TEA, it is the CUP we must find."

"Of course!" they all said at once.

"It was a white cup with a ring of pink bats around it," said Dorrie.

They rushed off to find the cup. They looked at the teacups the witches and wizards were holding.

They looked and looked and looked.

Suddenly they saw it. The nice fat witch in sunglasses had it in her hand.

When the fat witch saw them running toward her, she gave a shriek and leaped into the air.

The cup sailed out of her hands.

Dorrie made a big jump into the air. She got the cup just before it could smash on the floor.

"Yow!" said Dorrie. "I'm glad I caught it."

Dorrie held the cup very carefully in her hands and sat down.

Mr. Obs got the fat witch another cup of tea. They all said they were sorry they scared her.

The fat witch in sunglasses sat down beside Dorrie.

"What is so special about that cup, my dear?" asked the fat witch.

"It's not just a cup," said Dorrie. "It's my mother. Wink the Wizard played a mean trick."

The fat witch in sunglasses looked at Dorrie and Mr. Obs and Squig and Dinger and Miss Dorp.

"I know a secret," she whispered. "I know a secret about Wink the Wizard that nobody else knows. I know because my cousin has a friend who has an uncle who has a niece who used to be Wink's cook. Tell me, my dear, can you make fudge?"

Dorrie shook her head. "I'm not allowed to use the stove. And Cook is away."

The fat witch got up. "I will help you. Wink cannot resist fudge."

"Oh," said Dorrie. "I hope it will work."

They all hurried outside to get their broomsticks.

Dorrie and Gink went with the fat witch, and everyone flew away to Dorrie's house.

Dorrie put on an apron. She got out pots and pans, and sugar and milk and butter and chocolate.

Dorrie and the fat witch mixed up a big, big, big pot
of fudge.

Squig opened the door so the smell of the fudge would float skyward.

The kitchen grew dark as the fudge slowly cooked.

They poured it into a big pan to let it cool and then they sat very still and waited.

"Shhhhh," said the fat witch, "I hear him!"

There was a swish of air outside the door. And suddenly a dark shape grabbed for the pan of fudge. Squig slammed the door and locked it.

Everybody else jumped on top of Wink.

"Fudge! Fudge! Fudge!" mumbled Wink the Wizard.

"I want my mother back," said Dorrie. "As soon as you turn this teacup into the Big Witch, you can have the fudge. You can have the whole pan of fudge all for yourself."

Wink the Wizard licked his lips. "All of it? I'll do it. Anything, anything at all. You want a witch instead of a teacup. So it shall be."

Wink took some magic dust out of his sleeve and dropped it into the cup. He mumbled and spun three times.

There was a POUF!

Wink the Wizard and the pan of fudge disappeared.

There stood the Big Witch with a big smile, and her arms around Dorrie.

All that was left of the spell was a small ring of
pink bats around the Big Witch's hat.

"I'm so glad you're home," said Dorrie.

"Me, too," said the Big Witch. "Thank you for saving me from the Wizard's spell."

The Big Witch made a big jug of hot cocoa. They all put on their ice skates and went skating on the pond in the moonlight.

Afterwards, they built a fire and sat around and sang songs until it was time for bed.